MY HAMSTER'S GOT

TALENT

Books by Dave Lowe

The Stinky and Jinks series
My Hamster Is a Genius
My Hamster Is a Spy
My Hamster Is an Astronaut
My Hamster's Got Talent

Coming soon
My Hamster Is a Pirate
My Hamster Is a Detective

The Incredible Dadventure
The Mumbelievable Challenge
The Spectacular Holly-Day

MY HAMSTER'S GOT

TALENT

DAVE LOWE

ILLUSTRATED BY THE BOY FITZ HAMMOND

Piccadilly
P R E S S

First published in Great Britain in 2012 by
TEMPLAR PUBLISHING

This edition published in 2018 by
PICCADILLY PRESS
80–81 Wimpole St, London W1G 9RE
www.piccadillypress.co.uk

A CIP catalogue record for this book is available
from the British Library.

ISBN: 978-1-84812-658-9
Also available as an ebook

1

Printed a ... S.p.A.

Pi

To my mum and dad, who took me to the library.

THE JINKS FAMILY
Me, Lucy, Mum Dad and Stinky

Chapter 1

We were having our tea when my little sister, Lucy, pulled a leaflet out of her pocket, unfolded it and put it on the table so we could all read it.

'I got it from school,' she said, beaming with excitement.

THE PET SOCIETY PET SHOW
PRIZES FOR...

- Best Dog in Show
- Best Cat in Show
- Dog Obedience
- Most Talented Pet

'I will be entering Delilah into the cat show,' she announced breathlessly.

Delilah was the ginger kitten that Lucy had got for her seventh birthday, two weeks ago. That cat was now pretty much the only thing that my sister ever talked about. It was a rare sentence of Lucy's that didn't include the word 'Delilah'.

'Could you make an outfit for Delilah, Mum?' she asked.

Mum's speciality was making costumes.

'I'm sorry, Lucy,' my mum said, 'but cats don't really like to be dressed up.'

'Unless it's in a *catsuit*,' said my dad, whose speciality was making truly terrible jokes. 'Or you could make her wear a hat, so she'd be *a cat in a hat*. Or a pair of mittens, and then she'd be . . .'

'A kitten in mittens,' I groaned.

Mum gave Dad one of her regular 'stop-making jokes' stares and then turned to Lucy.

'How about I make a pretty bow for her to wear?'

Lucy nodded. 'Delilah would love that,' she said.

'A bow sounds purr-fect,' Dad added, unable to stop himself. 'Get it? *Purr*-fect!'

We all sighed and, before he could make any more pathetic cat-based jokes, I said, 'I want to take Stinky to the pet show too.'

'To watch?' Lucy asked, frowning.

'No – to compete.'

Lucy giggled. 'There's no "best hamster" section, silly,' she said. 'Or "smelliest rodent".'

'But there is a "most talented pet" section,' I pointed out. 'And Stinky will win it.'

Now *all* of them burst out laughing, as if I'd just told them a brilliant joke.

My family thought that Stinky was just a

normal pet hamster, you see. Only *I* knew that he was a genius.

'What's his special talent?' Lucy asked with a snort. 'Pooing?'

'He's a very good sleeper too,' my dad added, chuckling.

My mum glared at Dad and Lucy.

'Don't listen to them, Ben. Stinky's a really nice hamster. Although I'm not sure you could call him *talented* exactly. What tricks can he do?'

I hesitated. Stinky had hundreds of amazing talents. He was brilliant at maths, for example, and fluent in several languages. He knew pretty much *everything* about *everything*, to be honest.

The problem was, I couldn't tell Mum about any of this, because Stinky wanted it all kept a secret – even from my family.

'So, what *is* his special talent?' Lucy asked, wide eyed.

'You'll see,' I said.

Chapter 2

I put the leaflet on my desk next to Stinky's cage and, when he'd finished reading it, I said, 'What could your talent be?'

'That's a difficult question,' he said, 'because I'm rather good at so many different things.'

He wasn't very modest, for a hamster.

'There is a problem, however,' he continued. 'If I *do* enter the competition, my performance will be so astounding that people will realise I'm a genius. So, no talking. No maths. No dazzling the crowd with my knowledge. Anyway, who says I *want* to be in a talent show?'

'There are cash prizes,' I said. 'And I know just the thing I could buy for you.'

I went over to my drawer, picked out a small cutting from a magazine and showed it to him.

HAPPY HAMSTER BALL
HOURS OF EXERCISE
AND FUN FOR YOUR PET

Stinky didn't look too impressed though.

'So, let me get this straight,' he said. 'If I win the talent show, I get to be shut up inside a clear plastic ball?'

'Look at the hamster in the picture,' I said.

*Hamster Not included

'He's having a *great* time.'

'Or, more likely,' Stinky argued, 'he's in a state of complete shock from being stuck in a plastic prison from which there is no escape.'

I sighed. 'If you don't want a hamster ball,' I said sulkily, 'I could always get you something else with the prize money – a bigger cage, for example. Some tubes to make a burrow. Anything.'

He seemed a bit more interested now. He took another look at the leaflet, scrunched up his forehead in concentration and then his nose twitched. This usually meant he'd had a great idea.

'Do you know what "dog obedience" is?' he asked me.

'I'm sorry to tell you this, Stinky, but you're not a dog.'

He frowned at me impatiently. 'Dog obedience,' he explained, 'is when the dog's owner says ,"Sit!" and the dog sits. And then the owner tells the dog to roll over or stay or fetch, and the dog does those things.'

'Oh yeah,' I said. 'I've seen that. It's pretty cool.'

'Dogs are very silly animals like that,' said Stinky. 'Tell them to do something, and – if they can understand it – they'll usually do it. To my knowledge, however, no one has ever trained a *hamster* before. So, for the pet show, we could do "hamster obedience". Then *you* would actually look like the clever one, Ben. I'd just look like a regular hamster that had been brilliantly trained.'

I grinned. It was a fantastic idea.

'What are we waiting for?' I said excitedly. 'Let's practise right now!'

'I'm actually rather tired,' he complained.

'Come on, Stinky. Just for a minute.'

'If we must,' he sighed.

So I said, 'Sit!' and he sat.

'Roll over!' I said, and he did that too, although not very enthusiastically. 'You *could* do it with a bit more energy,' I said.

'I am trying to avoid rolling in my own poo,' he snapped. 'Because a certain *someone* hasn't cleaned out my cage for a while.

I sighed. Nothing was ever easy with Stinky.

'Fetch!' I said.

'Fetch what?' he asked.

'Fetch – I don't know . . . some carrot.'

He glanced at the piece of carrot over on the other side of his cage and then looked back at me and shook his head.

'Why not?' I asked, frowning.

'I *always* eat over on *that* side of the cage,' he said. 'Why on earth would I want to bring the carrot over here, near to where I poo? It's unhygienic.'

'It's called hamster obedience,' I said. 'Not hamster *dis*obedience.'

He nodded. 'That's an excellent point,' he said. 'And, on the day of the competition, I will do whatever you ask me to, I promise.'

'In that case,' I said, 'we'll win for sure! What could possibly beat a hamster doing tricks?'

At school the next day, I found out.

Chapter 3

Miss Miles was my teacher, but everyone called her Miss *Smiles* because she was usually so happy.

She knew all about the pet show. She'd stuck up a poster in class and asked if we had any pets.

Most of us *did* have pets, and she wanted to know what kinds of animals they were.

Some people had cats, some had dogs. Stuey Jones had a goldfish called Richard. Grace Short (who *is* very short) had a really long snake called Boris. There were guinea pigs and birds too. Edward Eggington – my next-door neighbour and number-one enemy – had five white mice. But I was the only one with a hamster.

'As you can all see from the poster,' Miss Miles said, 'there's a "talented pet" section of the show. Now, who can tell me what a talent is?'

Edward Eggington's hand shot up. His hand was up so often that his shoulder must have been sore at the end of every day.

'A talent is something you're good at,' he explained. 'For example, *I'm* talented at maths and science and writing, etcetera. Benjamin

Jinks is talented at getting the wrong answers and picking his nose.'

Most of the class giggled. But not me, and not Miss Miles.

'Another talent, Edward,' she said, frowning, 'is being nice to others – and that's certainly not a talent you're demonstrating at the moment.'

Then she spoke to the whole class.

'Every animal, just like *each* of you, has their own special talent. For example, did you know that a kangaroo could jump from one end of this classroom to the other in a single leap?'

Judging by the gasps in the room, most of us hadn't known this.

'Did you also know,' she continued, 'that

chameleons can change their skin colour to hide from other animals? And that rabbits can see in front *and* behind at the same time, so they can tell if something scary is coming from any direction?'

More gasps.

Stuey Jones had his hand up.

'Yes, Stuart?'

'If there was an animal that was half-rabbit, half-chameleon,' he said, 'it would be brilliant at hide-and-seek, miss.'

Everyone laughed, including Miss Miles.

'Now,' she said, 'what special talents do *your* pets have?'

Lots of hands went up. There were dogs that were good at fetching things or catching

Frisbees, and cats that were excellent hunters.

Grace Short's snake could wrap itself around her shoulders like a wriggly scarf.

Stuey Jones had his hand up again too. 'My fish, Richard, is very good at swimming, miss.'

'I should hope so,' Miss Miles said.

'My dog,' said Riley Green, 'is really good at farting.' Riley was actually pretty talented at that himself. 'They're very loud and very,

very smelly,' he explained.

Everyone giggled.

'I'm not sure that's something to be proud of, Riley,' Miss Miles said, rolling her eyes. 'And certainly not for the talent competition. Are any of you actually thinking of entering your pet into the show?'

This time, only me and Edward Eggington put our hands up.

'What can your hamster do, Ben?' she asked.

'He can sit and roll over, and fetch things, miss.'

'A *hamster* can do all those things?'

'Yes, miss.'

'Gosh. He sounds very talented indeed.

And what about your mice, Edward? What can they do?'

'I'm training them to do gymnastics,' he said. 'Me and my dad, who's a scientist.'

Every day Edward would find a way to mention that his dad was a scientist.

'Gymnastic mice?' said Miss Miles, wide-eyed.

'They perform amazing tricks – not only rolling over, but also jumping and balancing. They can even make a mouse-pyramid, standing on each other's backs.'

He looked at me and gave an evil grin. 'They'll be absolutely unbeatable,' he whispered.

Chapter 4

After tea, Stinky and I were watching TV in my room. Our favourite show, *Spy Gang*, had just been on, and now there was a wildlife documentary about lions. On the screen, a lion had chased down a gazelle and was tucking into it.

'Do lions eat hamsters?' I asked Stinky. 'For a snack, I mean. Between meals.'

'Fortunately for us,' he said, 'we usually live in different places.'

'Oh. Of course,' I said. 'Lions live in the

jungle. Hamsters live in pet shops and kids' bedrooms.'

He sighed. 'That's not what I meant. Hamsters live in the wild too, you know. We just don't usually live near lions, thank goodness.'

I found it hard to imagine Stinky living in the wild. He wasn't a big fan of going outside, full stop, and he'd told me before that lots of animals would like to eat hamsters, given the chance.

'So, when hamsters live outdoors,' I asked him, 'how do they survive?'

'We dig burrows,' he explained, 'and live underground quite a lot of the time, so nothing can get to us. We even dig different rooms in our burrows. A place for eating, a place for sleeping, a toilet.'

'Like an underground house?'

'Exactly.'

'So hamsters *are* talented,' I said, and then added glumly, 'just not quite as talented as a bunch of mice.'

Stinky frowned at me. 'I am not about to be beaten by a team of gymnastic mice,' he said.

Then he had an idea. His nose twitched excitedly and his eyes brightened.

'Bring me your toy box, Ben.'

I dragged it out from under my bed. Inside were lots of things I hardly played with any more – old teddies, building blocks, cars.

Stinky pointed out two things – a toy car and a box of dominoes.

'Are you sure?' I said. 'You told me you never wanted to play me at dominoes ever again. Or draughts. Or *anything* really. In fact, you said that playing games against a slug would be more of a challenge.'

'I was right,' he said. 'And it wouldn't have to be a high-achieving slug either. However, I don't want to *play* dominoes. I just need

one domino, the wheels from that car, some scissors and some sticky tape.'

'What for?'

'You'll see.'

Of course, hamsters, even genius ones, can't hold scissors or use sticky tape – their paws are much too tiny. So Stinky barked instructions at me through the bars of his cage and sat there supervising while I did all the work.

After a long time of me snipping, sticking and making tiny adjustments, Stinky finally told me that he was happy with it.

I stared at what I'd made, and then frowned at Stinky.

'What is it?' I asked him.

'What does it look like?'

'It looks like a domino with wheels,' I said.

'It's a *skateboard*,' he said. 'For me. Because if there's one thing more spectacular than gymnastic mice, it's a hamster on a skateboard, don't you think?'

I whooped. He was right!

'Hang on,' I said. 'Do you even know how to skate?

'Not yet,' he admitted. 'But even you can do it. So how difficult can it be?'

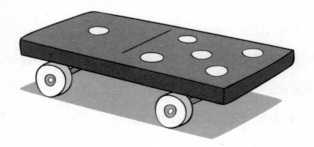

Chapter 5

Stinky asked me to lift him out of his cage so he could practise on my desk but, as soon as he got on the skateboard, he lost his balance and landed on his bottom.

He muttered, shook his head and stepped back onto the board.

Then he wobbled, yelped and fell off again.

'Ouch,' he said.

At school today, after we'd learned about special animal talents, Miss Miles told us about things that some animals *can't* do.

Kangaroos, for example, can't walk backwards. Cows can't walk down stairs (which explains why you never see one in a basement). Elephants can't jump.

She should have added something else to that list: hamsters can't skate.

It was ten minutes before Stinky could get the skateboard moving, but then the problem was he couldn't *stop*. I had to catch him before he fell off the desk and plummeted to the floor. I put him back on the desk and he tried to get his breath back.

'Skateboarding,' he complained, 'is by no means as easy as it looks.'

'We can give up if you want,' I said with a shrug, 'and try something else.'

'Give up?' Stinky wheezed, as if he didn't even understand the meaning of the words. 'I think not.'

He hopped back onto the skateboard. And fell off again.

Just *watching* him was painful.

'I've got an idea, Stinky.'

He looked up at me suspiciously. 'When *you* have an idea,' he said, 'it usually ends up with *me* doing something highly dangerous.'

'Not this time,' I said. 'I've learned a lot from you, Stinky. But today I'm going to try to teach *you* something.'

I put him back in his cage and then moved it next to my window, so he had a good view of the garden. Then I went outside, fetched my skateboard from the shed and put on my helmet.

I wasn't fantastic at skateboarding but,

unlike Stinky, I at least knew how to stay on the thing, most of the time.

I skated around the garden, showing Stinky how to go fast, how to turn and how to stop without hurting himself. Then I showed him a couple of tricks: I spun around, did a little jump and finally flipped up the skateboard and caught it.

When I'd finished I looked at Stinky and gave him a thumbs up.

Hamsters don't have thumbs, of course, and he couldn't give me one back. So I rushed straight back to my room to find out if my demonstration had been useful.

'What did you think?' I panted.

'Most instructive,' he said.

'Excuse me?'

He sighed. 'It means *I learned a lot.*'

'Oh,' I said. 'Good.'

Chapter 6

'**A**re you absolutely sure this is safe?' my mum asked me again.

The four of us – Mum, Dad, Lucy and me – were sitting around the kitchen table, but it wasn't teatime. It was *show* time.

Stinky was on the table, next to his little skateboard.

Mum and Dad wanted to see what Stinky could do, before deciding whether to enter him into the pet show. Because, when I'd told them that he could skate, they didn't believe me.

I couldn't blame them. I had a bit of a history of telling little fibs. Like the time I told them I'd seen a man-eating python in the garden, and it turned out to be a slightly-bigger-than-average worm.

My mum frowned at Stinky and the skateboard. 'This might be animal cruelty,' she said.

'He's wearing a crash helmet,' I pointed out. It was the one I'd made him when he'd been an astronaut.

'Crash helmet?' scoffed my dad. 'It's just half a ping-pong ball. That won't be much help when he plummets off the table and lands head first on the floor.'

'Poor little thing,' said Lucy. 'It *is* cruel.'

'You once dressed him up in a doll's bikini,' I said. '*That's* what I call animal cruelty.'

Stinky must have got fed up hearing us argue, because he'd already stepped onto the board and had started skating.

We all went quiet as he zoomed towards the edge of the table.

But when it looked like he wasn't going to stop, Lucy squealed, Mum gasped and Dad cupped his hands just below the table's edge, like a cricketer waiting for a catch.

I was really calm though.

I'd watched Stinky do this hundreds of times on my desk.

Now, just as he reached the edge, he skidded spectacularly to a stop, flicked up the skateboard, spun around and skated back to where he started.

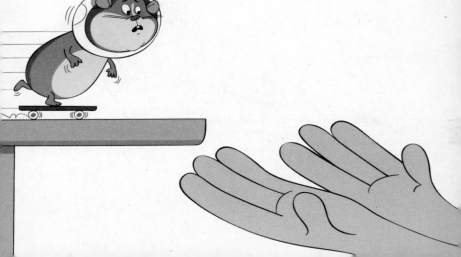

My mum sighed with relief.

My dad stared, wide-eyed, and said, 'Wow!'

Lucy, for a change, was speechless.

'Wait until you see this,' I said, as I put a ramp on the table. Well, it was actually a doorstop, but Stinky used it like a ramp, and did a couple of amazing jumps.

When Stinky's show finished, my whole family gave him a round of applause, and then Dad turned to me.

'How on earth did you teach him to do *that*?' he asked.

The truth was, I'd only shown Stinky how to skate once. After that he had improved all by himself. Every day when I went to school, I left the skateboard in his cage so he could practise. Every evening I put him on my desk so he had a lot more space to work in, and he practised some more.

'That little hamster,' my dad said, 'has a brain the size of a *pea*. And yet you, Ben, taught him how to do tricks on a skateboard. Incredible!'

'So he can enter the competition?' I asked.

'Of course he can!' said Dad. 'He might even win it!'

Chapter 7

On the morning of the pet show, the whole family got up early.

Mum and Lucy spent ages grooming Delilah. Judging by the screechy cat noises coming from Lucy's bedroom, Delilah wasn't a huge fan of having her fur combed.

My dad was so excited by Stinky's skateboarding performance in the kitchen that he was fiddling with his phone, working out how to use the video camera function so he could film the talent show. Dad usually had trouble working the *kettle*, so it was anyone's guess if he'd actually be able to record anything.

He was in the front room now, trying to figure it out.

Meanwhile, I was watching Stinky do some last-minute preparation. He was on my desk, practising his favourite trick – the one where

he jumped up, spun the skateboard, then landed back on it and kept going. But this time he missed the skateboard completely and landed on the desk with a thud.

I looked at him, shocked. He *always* got that trick right.

'Are you feeling OK, Stinky?'

He got to his feet, shook himself and muttered something that I couldn't make out.

'What happened?' I said. 'Are you nervous?'

He glared at me. 'In a few hours,' he snapped, 'I will be performing in front of a considerable audience. Wouldn't *you* be nervous?'

I nodded. '*I'm* nervous practically all of the time,' I told him. 'I'm nervous when I'm playing sports, when I'm talking to a grown-up, when

Miss Miles asks me a question in class. Lucy used to be even worse – she'd get really, really nervous just before she danced in front of people. She'd get stage fright, so badly that she'd actually be shaking. But then Dad gave her some really good advice.'

EEEK!!!

Stinky snorted. 'I find it extremely hard to believe that advice from your dad could help *anyone*,' he said. He was probably still annoyed about being called pea-brained.

'He told her to imagine that everyone in the audience was in their undies,' I explained. 'It sounds crazy, but it really helped her to calm down.

Stinky shuddered. 'Imagining *your dad* in his underwear is unpleasant enough,' he said. 'I think I'd rather be a complete bag of nerves than have *that* image in my mind.'

Chapter 8

In the car on the way to the show, Lucy had a special cat box on her lap, with Delilah inside. Lucy had fluffed up Delilah's fur so much that she looked less like a cat and more like a huge ball of fur.

Stinky was on *my* lap, in his cage. Whenever I'd travelled with him before, I'd taken him in a lunchbox, but he was much happier in his cage.

When we arrived, my dad filmed absolutely everything – he filmed us getting out of the car, he filmed us making our way through the big crowd at the pet show. He even filmed my mum as she was  telling him to stop filming.

The pet show was at the big school, and most of the things were going on inside: the dog competition was in the gym and the cat contest in the main hall, which is where Mum and Lucy took Delilah.

The Talented Pet competition, however, was in a big marquee on the school field, so me and Dad went over there. I was carrying Stinky

in the cage, trying not to rattle it (or rattle *him*).

An important-looking lady was sitting at a very long table, and I walked nervously over to her. A card on the table in front of the lady said 'Beverley Best – Judge'.

'Yes?' she said impatiently.

'I want to enter my hamster into the competition, please.'

'Name?'

'My name, or his name?'

'Both.'

'My name is Ben – Benjamin Jinks.' I held out the cage. 'And this here is Jasper Stinkybottom.'

When she heard his name, she pulled a face like she'd just been sucking on a lemon.

'We call him "Stinky" for short,' I added, as if that might help.

It didn't.

She grimaced again and wrote both our names down.

'I'm not sure I want to ask,' she said, 'but what is his particular talent?'

'Skateboarding,' I said proudly.

She stared at me for a few seconds.

'Well, now I've heard everything,' she said. 'Put "Stinky" . . .' she pulled another face, 'on the table with all the other small animals.'

I found an empty place on the table, next to the cage holding Edward Eggington's mice. The inside of their cage was decorated like a gym, with a little blue mat and a tiny springboard and beam. Edward Eggington was leaning over the cage, making final preparations, when he noticed me. He clearly hadn't forgiven me for beating him in the science competition.

'If it isn't Benjamin Jinks and his Hopeless Hamster,' he sneered.

'*Skateboarding* Hamster, actually,' I said. 'And I think he's got a really good chance of winning.'

For a few moments Edward looked worried, but then he glared at me.

'That hamster,' he said, 'has absolutely no chance.'

Chapter 9

The first contestant was a yappy little dog called Brock, who stood up on his back legs, walked around a bit and then shook paws with his owner. Everyone clapped.

Next was Polly the Polite Parrot. Her owner was an old lady who beamed proudly as Polly squawked, 'Excuse me, please,' then, 'Thank you very much,' and, 'You're welcome.'

My dad was standing next to me, filming everything.

'That bird has better manners than my kids,' I heard him mutter.

I sighed and wished that Stinky could talk when it was his turn. That parrot only knew a few words – my hamster knew a few *languages*. Though he hardly ever said 'please' or 'thank you' in any of them.

Next came a guinea pig called Brian who could hurdle pencil cases, and then a rat called Cuddles who chased his own tail (but never quite caught it, unfortunately).

Edward Eggington had been standing next to the mouse cage during the other performances, getting everything ready, and now it was *his* turn.

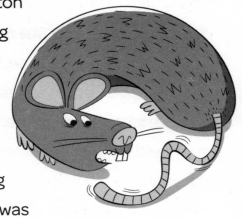

He coughed to get everyone's attention and then announced in a big voice:

'Ladies and gentlemen, I proudly present the Most Talented Mice in the Entire World, performing incredible gymnastic feats!'

He pulled a shiny whistle from his pocket and blew it. The mice all rolled over at the same time. The audience clapped wildly.

When the audience was quiet, Edward blew the whistle twice. The time the mice formed a line and – one by one – leaped up from the springboard onto the beam, walked carefully along it and jumped off spectacularly.

The audience gasped.

Finally he whistled three times – peep-peep-**peeeep** – and the mice climbed on each other's backs to make a mouse-pyramid.

When the mouse at the top took a bow, there was a huge cheer. Even my dad was clapping, which is not an easy thing to do with a phone in one hand.

Edward Eggington looked even more

pleased with himself than he usually did. He waved to the crowd with both arms in the air, as if he'd already won.

Maybe he had.

I had to admit, it was an impressive performance.

I just hoped that Stinky wouldn't get stage fright, because he'd have to be absolutely brilliant to beat those mice. I wondered how he was feeling. He'd been incredibly nervous at home – how would he feel when he saw the big audience staring at him?

I looked at his cage, but couldn't see him – he must have been in his little house, no doubt preparing himself mentally.

When the applause finally died down,

Beverley Best got everyone's attention. 'Our next contestants,' she announced, 'are Benjamin Jinks and . . .' she sighed, '*Stinky* the Skateboarding Hamster.'

I took a deep breath and walked up to the table.

But when I looked in Stinky's cage, suddenly I couldn't breathe.

The little house was empty.

Stinky wasn't there.

It was a few seconds before I could squeeze any words out.

'He's gone!' I yelled.

The audience gasped.

'It must be Stinky the *Invisible* Hamster,' Edward Eggington called out.

My dad stopped filming and rushed straight over to me.

We both looked desperately around for Stinky – on the table, on the ground.

But he was absolutely nowhere to be seen.

Chapter 10

When most of the other people and their pets had gone home, we were still there.

The sun was setting and the pet show was long over. Delilah had come fifth in the cat show. Edward Eggington's mice had won the

talent show. But none of that mattered. It didn't matter at all.

I was calling Stinky's name over and over. We'd looked everywhere in the Talented Pet marquee and now we were combing the field behind it. Delilah was sleeping inside her box on the grass, and Mum and Lucy had joined Dad and me and a few other helpful people on our search. We spread out, treading slowly and looking carefully, but there was no sign of my hamster.

What had happened to him? Had he got so nervous that he'd opened the cage by himself and run away? Had the pressure got too much for him?

I was blinking a lot to try to stop myself crying, but it was no good. A sick feeling in my tummy told me that Stinky wasn't coming back.

Dad came over to me and put his arm around my shoulder.

'It's getting dark, Ben,' he said softly. 'I think it's time to give up.'

I shook my head and dabbed at my tears with a sleeve.

'Give up?' I said. 'No way! Stinky wouldn't give up, so I'm not going to either.'

'Look,' said Dad, very gently, 'I'm really sorry, but I think he's probably gone, Ben.'

We kept on walking though, keeping our eyes on the ground for any sign of Stinky.

'I know it won't be the same, but we can always get another hamster,' my dad added.

'I don't *want* another hamster,' I whimpered.

Lucy and Mum had walked over to us by

now. Lucy gave me a hug.

'You can share Delilah with me,' she said.

'I don't want to share Delilah,' I muttered. 'I want Stinky back.'

Then my mum hugged me too.

I suppose it was nice that everyone wanted to give me a hug, but I just wanted to be left alone. Besides, instead of hugging, we should all have been looking for Stinky.

Finally it got too dark to see anything and we trudged back to the car and drove home in silence.

When we got back, I went straight to my room and threw myself on the bed.

Dad came in soon after and sat on the edge of my bed. 'Poor Stinky,' he said, looking at the empty cage on my desk. 'Poor you.'

I was too upset to speak.

'How on earth did he escape anyway?' Dad said. 'That's what I can't understand. The cage was closed.'

After he'd left, I thought about what he'd said. How *had* Stinky got out? Where had he gone? *Had* he escaped, or was it possible that he'd been stolen?

Stinky would have been able to work out the answers to these questions. But that was the problem.

Stinky

wasn't here.

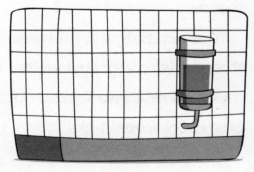

Chapter 11

Usually it was Stinky who woke me up. Sometimes it was the sound of him nibbling noisily on grain or running around on his wheel. Sometimes it was him complaining that I hadn't cleaned out his cage.

But this time it wasn't Stinky, it was an *idea* that got me out of bed.

I rushed straight to my parents' room, where they were both still sleeping. I went over to my dad's side and rocked his shoulder till he opened his eyes.

'What is it?' he grunted.

'I need to watch what you filmed yesterday, Dad,' I whispered.

He grunted again. 'Can't it wait?' he murmured. 'I was dreaming about a nice plate of sausages and eggs and I want to get right back to it.'

He closed his eyes.

'I need your help to find Stinky, Dad,' I whispered. 'If he's still alive.'

He opened his eyes again and looked sadly at me. 'I'm really sorry, but that's a big "if", Ben,' he mumbled. But he got up anyway and we stood in the hall as Dad fumbled with his phone and played the talent-show footage.

His camerawork was pretty shaky, but you could just about make out what was going on.

First there was the little dog walking on his back legs, and then came the parrot.

'That bird could teach you and Lucy a thing or two about being polite, that's for sure,' my dad said.

As the parrot was performing, though, something else on the screen caught my eye.

Actually it was someone: Edward Eggington was lurking in the background at the corner of the screen. At first he was just checking on his mice, but then I saw his hands move.

They moved over to Stinky's cage.

And, in one quick movement, he opened the cage, scooped Stinky out, *tossed him onto the grass* and then calmly closed the cage door.

I gasped.

'What?' my dad said, turning to me.

I was speechless for a few seconds, but then all my words seemed to come out at once.

'Didn't-you-see-it?'

'See what? The parrot?'

'No!' I yelped. 'That's the problem! Everyone

at the show was watching the parrot,' I said. That's why nobody saw him!'

'Saw who?'

'Edward Eggington, of course! Rewind it! Play it back in slow motion!'

Eventually Dad managed to do this and, when it was replaying in slow motion, I went up to the screen so I could show him what had happened.

'That's Edward Eggington!' I said, pointing out the blurry figure in the background. 'That's him taking Stinky out of his cage!' I could hardly speak I was so furious. 'And *that's* him throwing Stinky onto the ground!'

My dad pressed pause.

He didn't get angry very often. But now his

face was red and his voice was wobbly with rage.

'Caught in the act!' he spluttered. 'What a terrible boy! That hamster was a member of our family! He will pay for this!'

But punishing Edward Eggington wouldn't get Stinky back. I took a deep breath.

'Press play again, Dad.'

He did. I stared at the screen and pointed out the tiny brown dot scurrying away out the back of the marquee.

'That's Stinky,' I said. 'Now we know what direction he ran off in at least.'

My dad looked at me sadly. 'We looked *everywhere* yesterday, for hours.' He sighed. 'Edward Eggington will be punished, Ben. We'll make absolutely sure of that. But I'm sorry to say that I don't think Stinky's coming back. Pet hamsters just can't survive in the wild.

'But what if we were looking in the wrong place, Dad?'

'We checked the whole field!' he said.

'But we were looking *on* the ground,' I said.

We should've been looking *under* it. Wild hamsters live in burrows.'

My dad shook his head. But he could see how important this was to me.

'Come on then, son,' he said. 'Let's go and have another look.'

Chapter 12

With Mum and Lucy still sleeping, me and Dad went looking for Stinky again.

When we got to the field, we walked in the same direction that we'd seen Stinky run off in.

'What are we looking for exactly?' Dad asked.

'A hole in the ground. A hamster-sized hole. The opening for a burrow.'

We'd been going for a few minutes when I saw a little hole just in front of me. I scrambled onto my hands and knees and stared into it.

'Stinky?' I called. 'Are you in there? It's Ben!'

I waited, but there was no answer and no movement at all.

So I got up and went on searching. There were more holes, and I called and looked in every one. But no sign of Stinky.

Then I spotted something on the grass – something round, very small and brown.

I wasn't certain, but it looked like one of Stinky's poos. I got down on my knees to study it more closely and I'd never been so happy to see a poo in my life. I sniffed it. It looked like one of his, but I couldn't be sure.

My dad gave me a funny look. 'Step away from the poo, son.'

'I think it's Stinky's,' I said.

'Or, more likely,' he said, 'a mouse or a rat or some other rodent who actually lives out here.'

I got up and we kept walking.

After a while, my dad turned to me again. 'I really don't think he would've come this far,' he said sadly. 'Stinky's only got tiny legs, remember.' When I looked over my shoulder to see how far we'd come, our car was just a speck in the distance. 'We should turn back,' he added.

But I knew my hamster better than anyone. Stinky wouldn't have stopped until he was safely away from all the people and animals at the pet show. Who knew how far he'd go?

'Just a bit further, Dad,' I pleaded

He nodded reluctantly, but it didn't take much longer for *me* to start losing hope too. I was still calling Stinky's name, but more and more desperately now.

'You know, Ben,' my dad started, 'it's hard, but sometimes you have to say goodbye.' He was using his serious voice – a voice he saved for very special occasions.

'When *I* was young,' he went on, 'I had a little black-and-white dog called Meg. We did everything together, me and Meg. She was the best dog ever – always bouncing around, chasing cats, having fun. And then she got old. We still spent lots of time together, but she didn't have the same energy any more.

She spent most of
the day dozing. Then
one day, just after my
thirteenth birthday, she
fell asleep. She didn't
wake up again. But even though Meg had died,'
my dad explained, 'she never left me, not
really, because I still remember her, even now.

She lives on in my memory. Do you see what I'm saying, Ben?'

I did, but it didn't make me feel any better. My dad walked away from me, still looking for Stinky, though I could tell his heart wasn't in it.

I stopped walking and took a deep breath.

'Goodbye, Stinky,' I whispered. And then, louder, **'Goodbye, Stinky!'** Finally I yelled it at the top of my voice:

'Goodbye, Stinky!'

And that's when I saw it – a small hole in the ground just in front of me, and something moving inside it.

I stared, open-mouthed.

A little nose poked out, and two tiny eyes blinked back at me.

'Stinky?' I said.

'Well, I don't see any other hamsters around here,' he muttered.

I whooped with joy.

'Hello, Stinky!' I yelled.

Chapter 13

My dad drove home really carefully because Stinky was cradled in my hands, looking tired and happy and relieved. That's how I felt too.

Stinky obviously couldn't talk to me in the car, because my dad would have heard him, but I could still tell *him* stuff.

'We saw what Edward Eggington did,' I said. 'Dad caught it on his camera.'

'That boy is in a world of trouble,' my dad muttered. 'Your mum will see to that all right.'

When Dad had called to tell her we'd found Stinky, she'd hooted with delight. But then he'd told her what our next-door neighbour had done, and she fell completely silent.

When my mum went quiet, it usually meant that someone was in big, big trouble.

Sure enough, by the time our car turned slowly into our street, there was a small crowd of people outside the Eggingtons' house. Edward was on his doorstep, between his parents, and all three Eggingtons were looking pale. Beverley Best, the lady from the pet show, was there too – my mum must have called her – and some neighbours had gathered, probably wondering what all the noise was about.

The noise was mostly coming from my mum. She was yelling, wagging her finger at Edward and looking as if she might explode with rage.

When my dad parked the car and we got out, everyone turned to look at us.

'Welcome home, Stinky!' Lucy squealed, and everyone cheered.

Well, everyone except the Eggingtons.

Beverley Best ordered Edward to bring her the Talented Pet certificate and the cheque she'd presented him with yesterday.

When he came back, she snatched them from him and gave them to my dad, because my hands were full with Stinky.

'That hamster,' she said to me, '*a common pet hamster*, survived a night in the wild. If *that's* not a talent, I don't know what is.'

I smiled, thanked Beverley Best and left all the commotion behind – my mum hadn't finished with Edward Eggington, not by a long way.

In my room, I put Stinky back in his cage and sat on my bed, exhausted but incredibly happy.

Stinky scurried straight over to the carrot in the corner of his cage and started nibbling hungrily.

'Incredible!' I said, beaming. 'You managed to win the contest after all. Even without skateboarding. So, what can I get you with the prize money? A hamster ball?'

He stopped eating carrot for a second and stared at me. 'Certainly not,' he said.

'How about a bigger cage?' I suggested. 'With lots of tubes for making a burrow.'

'I've had quite enough of burrows,' he said.

'So what *would* you like?'

'Carrots,' he said, 'of all shapes and sizes. Lots of them. I never, ever want to be hungry again. Why any animal would want to live in the wild is absolutely beyond me. It's cold.

It's frightening. And, furthermore, there's absolutely nothing to eat.'

'I thought hamsters ate bugs.'

'Not *this* hamster,' he snapped. 'Have you ever eaten a bug?'

'One time I was running with my mouth open and a fly flew in.'

'And was it tasty?'

'No,' I said. 'Not a bit.'

'Well then. Bugs aren't exactly my food of choice either. I much prefer carrots,' he said, and had another nibble.

'Welcome home,' I said.

He looked up at me.

'Thank you for not giving up on me,' he said.

'You taught me that,' I told him.

'Yes,' he said. 'I suppose I did.' Then he shook his head. 'A "common pet hamster" indeed,' he muttered.

I smiled. There was *nothing* common about Stinky.

THE END

Have you read the first
STINKY and JINKS
adventure?

Piccadilly
PRESS

Look out for more
STINKY and JINKS
adventures...

A STINKY and JINKS ADVENTURE

MY HAMSTER IS A

SPY

DAVE LOWE

ILLUSTRATED BY
THE BOY FITZ HAMMOND

Piccadilly
PRESS

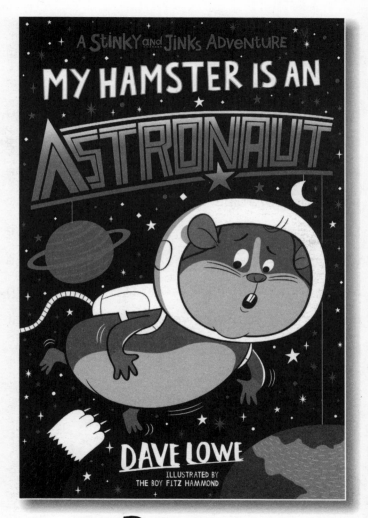

A Stinky and Jinks Adventure

MY HAMSTER IS AN

ASTRONAUT

DAVE LOWE

ILLUSTRATED BY
THE BOY FITZ HAMMOND

Piccadilly
PRESS

Dave Lowe grew up in Dudley in the West Midlands, and now lives in Brisbane, Australia, with his wife and two daughters. He spends his days writing books, drinking lots of tea, and treading on Lego that his daughters have left lying around. Dave's Stinky and Jinks books follow the adventures of a nine-year-old boy called Ben, and Stinky, Ben's genius pet hamster. (When Dave was younger, he had a pet hamster too. Unlike Stinky, however, Dave's hamster didn't often help him with his homework.) Find Dave online at @daveloweauthor or www.davelowebooks.com

Born in York in the late 1970s, **The Boy Fitz Hammond** now lives in Edinburgh with his wife and their two sons. A freelance illustrator for well over a decade, he loves to draw in a variety of styles, allowing him to work on a range of projects across all media. Find him online at www.nbillustration.co.uk/the-boy-fitz-hammond or on Twitter @tbfhDotCom

Thank you for choosing a Piccadilly Press book.

If you would like to know more about our authors, our books or if you'd just like to know what we're up to, you can find us online.

www.piccadillypress.co.uk

You can also find us on:

We hope to see you soon!